UNICORNS OF THE SECRET STABLE

Unicorn Uncovered

JOLLY FiSH PRESS

Mendota Heights, Minnesota

By Whitney Sanderson

Illustrated by Jomike Tejido

Book design by Sarah Taplin
Illustrations by Jomike Tejido
Illustration on page 35 by North Star Editions

Published in the United States by Jolly Fish Press, an imprint of North Star Editions, Inc.

First Edition
First Printing, 2020

This is a work of fiction. Names, characters, places, and incidents are either the product of the author's imagination or are used fictitiously, and any resemblance to actual persons living or dead, business establishments, events, or locales is entirely coincidental.

Library of Congress Cataloging-in-Publication Data (pending)
978-1-63163-404-8 (paperback)
978-1-63163-403-1 (hardcover)

Jolly Fish Press
North Star Editions, Inc.
2297 Waters Drive
Mendota Heights, MN 55120
www.jollyfishpress.com

Printed in the United States of America

TABLE OF CONTENTS

Welcome to Summerville

Home of Magic Moon Stable

Unicorn Guardians

A long time ago, unicorns and people lived together. When people started hunting the unicorns, two girls decided to help. They used unicorn magic to create a powerful spell. It closed off the Enchanted Realm from the rest of the world. Only the girls' keys could open the Magic Gate.

When the girls grew up, they gave the keys to their daughters. Since then, two young girls have always been the Unicorn Guardians.

CHAPTER 1

The Magic Gate

Ruby hurried across the yard. The silver key bounced on her chest as she ran. She passed the red barn and stopped in front of the wooden gate. A sign above it read, "Magic Moon Stable."

On the other side of the gate was an empty horse pasture. It was filled with weeds.

Ruby held up the key. On its handle was a gem the color of the summer sky. She put the key into the lock on the gate.

When Ruby stepped through the Magic Gate, she was not in a horse pasture. She was in a meadow filled with

wildflowers. Beyond the meadow was a

forest. Mountains rose tall and misty in

the distance.

And the meadow was not empty at all.

Starfire lifted his head from grazing. He galloped over and stopped in front of her.

"Good morning!" said Ruby. She scratched his forehead, beneath his horn. He had a bright-orange shooting star there, which held his magic.

"Hi, Ruby. Can you help me?" said a voice behind her.

Ruby turned and saw her sister, Iris. Iris's brown hair was neatly braided. Ruby's red hair was tangled. She'd been in too much of a hurry to brush it that morning.

"I think Winterlight hurt her leg," said Iris. "She will not hold still to let me look at it."

Ruby followed Iris across the meadow. The other unicorns lifted their heads in greeting. Some of them created swirls of stars with their horns. Unicorns did that when they were happy.

Winterlight was standing alone at the edge of the meadow. Her head hung low. She held one leg up off the ground. Ruby could see that she was in pain.

Ruby stood by Winterlight's head while Iris looked at the unicorn's leg.

"I see the problem," said Iris. "It's a thorn. Try to keep her still while I pull it out."

Ruby stroked Winterlight's neck. She told her how beautiful she was. Unicorns loved to be admired. The fancier you were about it, the better.

"Your mane is like silk," Ruby said.

"Your tail is like a cloud on a windy day."

Winterlight bobbed her head happily. Her ears went back when Iris pulled out the thorn.

"It's a big one," said Iris. She held it up. "Her leg is going to be sore."

Iris looked into the Fairy Forest beyond the meadow. The trees were so thick you could see only a short way into it.

"I'll gather some honey blossoms to make a balm," said Iris. "But I don't like going into the forest alone. Will you come with me?"

"Sorry. I can't," said Ruby. "I'm meeting Mia to ride bikes."

"Being a Guardian of the Enchanted Realm is a big responsibility," said Iris.

She was using her older-sister voice. "You should take it seriously."

"I *do* take it seriously," said Ruby. "But why can't one of the other unicorns heal Winterlight's leg?"

"Unicorn magic should only be used for serious problems," said Iris. "They can't use it for just any little thing."

Ruby looked back at the Magic Gate.

Mia must be wondering where she was.

"I will help you later," said Ruby. "I

promise." She waved goodbye and ran

across the pasture before Iris could

argue.

CHAPTER 2

A Big Crash

Ruby saw Mia's new lime-green bike as soon as she stepped through the Magic Gate. It was standing on its kickstand near the barn. But where was Mia?

Ruby walked into the barn. She found Mia in front of Casper's stall. The pony was so old that his fur was all white. Casper belonged to Mr. Jones, their neighbor.

"Hi, Mia!" said Ruby. "Sorry I'm late." She went over to Casper's stall and patted his shaggy neck.

"That's okay," said Mia. "You are always late!"

Ruby grabbed her bike from the empty stall next to Casper's. She put on and buckled her helmet. Then she followed Mia out of the barn.

The girls got on their bikes and took off down the street. Soon, they came to the center of Summerville.

The air smelled amazing as they passed

the Cupcake Castle. That was the bakery

their mom and aunt had just opened.

It was painted to look like a real castle.

The towers were giant frosted cupcakes.

Ruby wanted to stop for a snack.

But Mia was already way ahead of her,

pedaling fast.

Past the center of town was a brick

factory. Its chain-link gate swung open.

The yard was filled with old bricks,

boards, and barrels.

Mia stopped her bike. Her eyes lit

up. "We could make a great bike jump

with that stuff," she said, pointing.

"I saw a cool video online. Someone jumped their bike across a pit of lava!"

"That sounds like fun!" said Ruby.

Mia rode into the yard. "Help me build a ramp," she said.

Ruby put her kickstand down. "We can use these bricks and wood."

Once the ramp was complete, Mia put a piece of plastic pipe on the ground.

"Everything in front of that pipe is lava," she said. "I have to jump my bike to the other side."

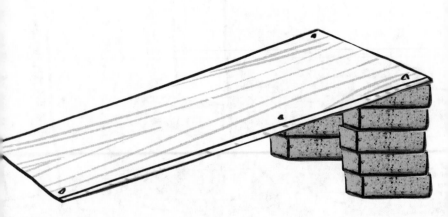

"That looks too far away," said Ruby.

"The person in the video jumped way

farther," Mia answered.

Mia's legs pumped as she rode up the ramp. For a second, Ruby thought she might make it. Then her front tire caught on a nail sticking up from the plywood.

The bike flipped over in midair, and Mia went flying.

CHAPTER 3

Unicorn Magic

Ruby watched as Mia lay asleep in the hospital bed. Mia's arm was in a sling. A big bandage covered her head.

Worst of all, she was not allowed to ride bikes for six weeks.

It's my fault, Ruby thought. *I helped build that ramp.*

Mia shared her hospital room with another patient. He was a boy named Nick. He sat in a wheelchair by the window. His leg was in a cast. He looked like he wanted to be playing outside.

Ruby slowly scratched her head. Sometimes, she had ideas. Crazy ideas.

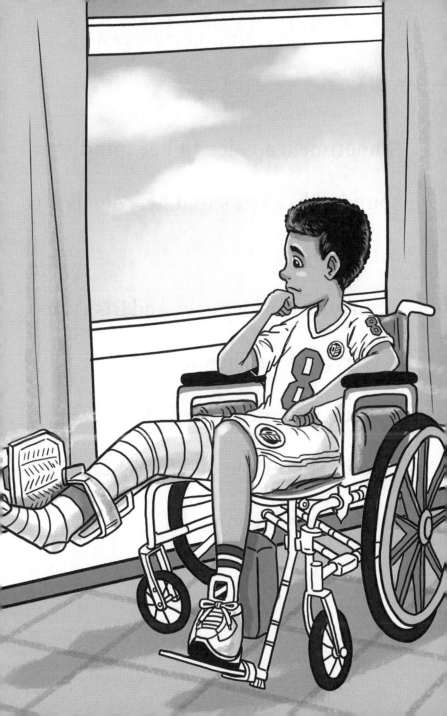

Sometimes, a voice in her mind that sounded like Iris's told her, *Absolutely not, no way, never.*

Ruby had an idea now. And Iris's voice was trying to tell her no.

But it was such a good idea . . .

Ruby slipped out of the hospital room and quickly ran home.

Unicorn Uncovered

When Ruby arrived back at the hospital, she did not go through the front door. Instead, she went around back and knocked on Mia's window. Nick wheeled his chair over to open it.

"Is that a horse wearing a top hat and a bow tie?" he asked. His eyes were bright and eager.

"His name is Starfire," said Ruby. "And he's actually a unicorn." She took off the top hat. "I had to put this on to hide his horn."

The people around town were used to Ruby doing funny things. Some of them had stared as she led Starfire through town. But no one had known he was a unicorn.

Nick's eyes widened. "Wow," he whispered. "Where did he come from?"

"Magic Moon Stable," Ruby answered. "He can heal your broken leg, if you want."

"That would be awesome," said Nick. "This cast itches so much."

Starfire stuck his head through the window. He gently touched his horn to the boy's shoulder. His horn glowed like moonlight.

"My leg doesn't hurt anymore!" said Nick.

"Can you wake Mia for me?" Ruby asked.

Nick gently shook Mia awake.

"Mia," Ruby said, "come over here." She motioned with her arms.

Mia yawned as she walked over to the window. When she saw Starfire, she rubbed her eyes. "Am I dreaming?"

"No," said Ruby. "We will be riding bikes again tomorrow!"

Starfire touched his horn to Mia's arm. A minute later, she took her arm out of the sling. She moved it all around.

Ruby smiled. It worked just like she thought it would. Unicorn magic could fix anything.

"Whoa!" Nick exclaimed a few minutes later. He was holding up his phone. "I took a video of Starfire healing Mia and posted it online. It already has more than five hundred views!"

CHAPTER 4

The Not-So-Secret Stable

The next morning, newspaper and TV reporters were waiting in front of Magic Moon Stable.

"We want to see the unicorn!" they cried. Their cameras flashed, even though Starfire was nowhere in sight.

Ruby gasped when she saw the reporters. She and Iris were on their way to the stable for their morning chores.

"What is going on?" asked Iris.

Ruby could not keep her secret any longer. She told Iris about the video.

"I know you were trying to help Mia and Nick," said Iris. "But our job is to protect the unicorns, not turn them into internet stars!"

"I'm sorry," said Ruby in a small voice. "I will fix this."

Ruby took a deep breath. She stood up straight. Then she cleared her throat. "Thank you all for coming," she said.

"Starfire needs to be brushed and fed. Come back this afternoon to meet him."

"Ruby, what are you doing?" Iris asked.

"Fixing this," Ruby said.

After Mia's accident, Ruby had looked up the video of the bike rider jumping over lava. She saw that the video had been made using special effects. It was a trick, a *hoax*.

She wasn't sure how, but Ruby had to

pull off a hoax too.

That afternoon, the reporters returned.

Ruby and Iris led them into the barn.

Mia and Nick were there too. "Here he is," said Ruby. She opened the stall door. "It's the magical unicorn, Starfire."

The reporters stared. They were quiet.

Casper took a bite of his hay and chewed. The horn that Ruby had made from an empty paper towel roll flopped sideways on his head.

"That's not the unicorn in the video!" said one reporter.

"It's definitely the same unicorn," said Ruby. "Did I mention that the video used special effects?"

The reporters looked at each other. They looked at Casper.

Casper shook his head. His fake horn fell off and landed in the hay.

"Well, I guess there is no story here," one of the reporters said. Suddenly, they were all leaving at once.

Iris gave Ruby a high five.

Mia stared at Casper. "Was it really just a trick?" she whispered. "It seemed so real."

Ruby felt guilty. But Iris was right. She was a Guardian. She had to keep the unicorns a secret.

"You did hit your head pretty hard," said Ruby.

"But what about my leg?" asked Nick. "It's not broken anymore."

"The power of positive thinking?" Ruby suggested.

Iris nodded and added, "I like to think that unicorns *are* real . . . but they just stay hidden."

Mia smiled. "Maybe. I would love to see a real one someday."

The next day, there were no stories about unicorns in the newspapers.

Everything was back to normal. But Ruby felt different. What if the hoax had not worked? What if the reporters had found their way into the Enchanted Realm?

Millions of people would have come to visit. They would leave trash. They would crush the flowers in the meadow. They would scare the unicorns.

Iris was right. Being a Guardian *was* a big responsibility. Ruby clutched her key tightly.

She was ready. Whatever it took, she would protect the unicorns.

THINK ABOUT IT

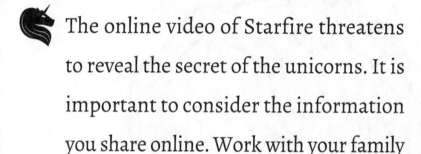

The online video of Starfire threatens to reveal the secret of the unicorns. It is important to consider the information you share online. Work with your family to set up rules about social media use.

Ruby and Mia construct a bike ramp to jump off. What are some things you like to do with your friends?

Ruby puts a fake horn on Casper to trick reporters. Write a list of three questions you can use to evaluate online videos.

ABOUT THE AUTHOR

Whitney Sanderson grew up riding horses as a member of a 4-H club and competing in local jumping and dressage shows. She has written several books in the Horse Diaries chapter book series. She is also the author of *Horse Rescue: Treasure,* based on her time volunteering at an equine rescue farm. She lives in Massachusetts.

ABOUT THE ILLUSTRATOR

Jomike Tejido is an author and illustrator of the picture book *There Was an Old Woman Who Lived in a Book.* He also illustrated the Pet Charms and My Magical Friends leveled reader series. He has fond memories of horseback riding as a kid and has always loved drawing magical creatures. Jomike lives in Manila with his wife, two daughters, and a chow chow named Oso.

RETURN TO MAGIC MOON STABLE

Book 1

Book 2

Book 3

Book 4

AVAILABLE NOW